Monday Popular Concerts.

DIRECTOR—Mr. S. ARTHUR CHAPPELL.

Four Hundred and Ninety-eighth Concert.*

PROGRAMME FROM THE WORKS OF

Various Masters.

MONDAY EVENING, JANUARY 11th, 1875.

Part I.

QUINTET, in A major, Op. 18, for two Violins, two Violas, and Violoncello. *Mendelssohn.*

(Seventh performance at the Popular Concerts.)

Allegro con moto—A major.
Intermezzo, andante sostenuto—F major.
Scherzo, allegro molto—D minor.
Allegro vivace—A major.

Herr STRAUS, Herr L. RIES, Mr. ZERBINI, Mr. BURNETT, and Signor PIATTI.

The Quintet in A major must always be a favourite with the lovers of Mendelssohn's music. The flowing, continuous, and gently expressive melody of the first *allegro*, the impetuous vigour of the last, the serene repose of the *andante*, the fine-wove texture and characteristic sprightliness of the *scherzo*, one of its composer's most individual and spontaneous creations, will hardly fail to excite the sympathy and rivet the interest of an audience which, "since the Popular Concerts became classical, and the Classical Concerts popular," has appreciated with invariable discrimination, and enjoyed with heartiness, the innumerable beauties by which the chamber-music of the great masters is distinguished. The Quintet, Op. 18, was composed in 1826, but not printed till six years

---

* Thirteenth Concert of the Seventeenth Session.

later. The *scherzo* was originally the second movement, the third movement being a minuet in F sharp (*allegro molto*), with a trio, in D—"*canone doppio*" (double canon.)* In 1832, when Mendelssohn was in Paris, he replaced the minuet and trio by the *intermezzo* which now immediately succeeds the first *allegro*. In the second volume of his "Letters" (Lady Wallace's translation) there is one, dated "*Paris*, Feb. 21st, 1832," in which the following passage occurs:—

"I have composed a grand *adagio*, as an *intermezzo* for the quintet. It is called 'Nachruf' (*adieux*); and it occurred to me, as I had to write something for Baillot, who plays so beautifully, is so kindly disposed towards me, and wishes to perform the quintet in public, although only a recent acquaintance.

In another letter, dated "*Paris*, Jan. 21st, 1832," we find a passing allusion to the same work:—

"It struck me that the Octet and the Quintet might make a very good appearance among my works, being in fact better than many compositions that already figure there. As the publication of these pieces costs me nothing, but, on the contrary, I derive profit from them, and not wishing to confuse their chronological order, my idea is to publish the following at Easter:—Quintet and Octet (the latter also arranged as a duet), *Midsummer Night's Dream*, *Seven Songs without Words*, *Six Songs with Words*; on my return to Germany, six pieces of sacred music, and finally, if I can get any one to print it, the Symphony in D minor, &c."

The reference to "chronological order" is curious, seeing that the Octet was composed in 1825, and the Quintet in 1826. The "Symphony in D minor," to which Mendelssohn very frequently alludes with evident interest, is the much talked of "*Reformation Symphony*," now, upwards of forty years later, famous both in the old world and the new.

The first movement of the Quintet in A major opens with the following tuneful and amply developed theme, the piquant harmony of which must speak for itself:—

Allegro con moto (first theme).

* These movements have never been published.

446

(Episode.)

(Second theme.)

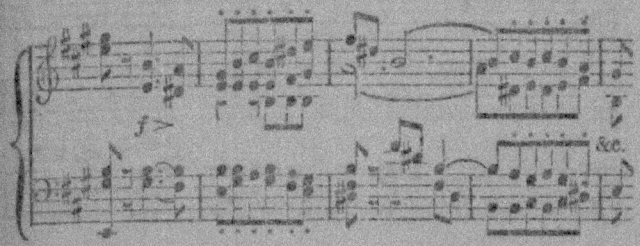

The pensive melody with which the *andante* composed for Baillot (*Nachruf*, as Mendelssohn calls it) sets out must also suffice without the harmony in which it is so richly clad:—

Andante sostenuto.

Scherzo (allegro molto).

1st Violin.

(Second theme.)

Finale (allegro vivace—melody only).

(Second theme—melody only.)

The principal tributaries of all four movements are equally striking; and indeed no real lover of Mendelssohn's music can be otherwise than interested in this quintet, which from one end to the other bears the strong impress of his genius. It was first introduced by Herr Molique, Herr L. Ries, Mr. Doyle, Herr Schreurs, and Signor Piatti, at the twelfth concert of the second season—Feb. 13, 1860.

NEW SONG, Miss EDITH WYNNE.   *Sullivan.*

"TENDER AND TRUE."

Could ye come back to me, Douglas, Douglas,
　In the old likeness that I knew,
I would be so faithful, so loving, Douglas,
　Douglas, Douglas, tender and true.

Never a scornful word should pain you,
　I'd smile as sweet as the angels do;
Sweet as your smile on me shone ever,
　Douglas, Douglas, tender and true.

Oh! to call back the days that are not!
　Mine eyes were blinded, your words were few;
Do you know the truth now, up in heaven,
　Douglas, Douglas, tender and true?

I was not half worthy of you, Douglas;
　Not half worthy the like of you!
Now, all men besides are to me like shadows,
　Douglas, Douglas, tender and true.

Stretch out your hand to me, Douglas, Douglas!
　Drop forgiveness from heaven like dew;
As I lay my heart on your dead heart, Douglas,
　Douglas, Douglas, tender and true.

———

3 z

PRELUDIO con FUGA (alla Tarantella), in A minor,
for Pianoforte alone.   J. S. Bach.

(Third performance at the Popular Concerts.)

Preludio, allegro moderato—A minor.
Fuga (alla Tarantella), vivace—A minor.

Madlle. MARIE KREBS.

The above composition, one of the most individual, remarkable, and difficult pieces ever composed for a keyed
instrument, forms No. 2, in Book 9, of F. C. Greipenkerl's
complete edition of the works of John Sebastian Bach for the
pianoforte, or, as it was called in his day, clavichord. Of the
eighteen original and beautiful pieces contained in Book 9 of
Greipenkerl's collection, only two had been engraved, until
that diligent enthusiast began his labour of collecting and
publishing. The Prelude and Fugue in A minor, now
introduced, was not one of these. It is barely alluded to
by Forkel, whose account of Bach and his writings is quite as
scanty as it is interesting. The most important epochs in the
artistic life of John Sebastian Bach were—*first*, his second
sojourn at Weimer, from 1708 to 1717 ; *second*, his engage-
ment at Coethen, from 1717 to 1825; and *third*, his es-
tablishment at Leipsic, as Director of the Music at St.
Thomas's Hospital, from 1723 until his death, on Feb. 28,
1750.* What Bach composed anterior to 1708 is of little
interest; but all he produced from that date onward is, as
Herr Greipenkerl justly remarks, "the property of the German
people"—or, as he might still more justly have remarked, of
the *civilized world*.

So far as we are enabled to judge from its style and
general character, the Prelude and Fugue in A minor (which
should not be confounded with the one more generally known†)

* At 8 o'clock in the evening—as Forkel informs us.

† The grand Fugue in A minor, one of the longest and most
difficult ever composed, and thus cursorily alluded to by Forkel:—
"As practice for the fingers of both hands, I particularly reckon a
fugue in A minor, in which the composer has taken great pains, by
an uninterrupted succession of running passages, to give to both
hands equal strength and facility." The same applies with not
less force to the Prelude and Fugue (*alla Tarantella*) now
introduced.

must have been composed before 1725.* It was therefore
one of the productions of the great musician's ripe maturity,
and—as Forkel well remarks—" contains numberless beauties
very nearly approaching the perfection of his later period."
That it was written merely " to augment the suppleness of
the composer's fingers"—as the same author suggests—it is
difficult to believe. The worthy biographer says nothing of the
picturesque beauty and original conduct of the prelude, nothing
of the wonderfully ingenious and masterly construction of the
fugue; and nothing (here, perhaps, not being a prophet, like
Bach himself, Forkel is hardly to be censured) of the fact,
that, both in prelude and fugue, the legitimate form of the
symphonic movement (as in the preludes of the *Suites An-
glaises*)—supposed to have been originated by Haydn—is
presented with a completeness and symmetry perfectly
astonishing, the period at which it is written taken into con-
sideration. The Prelude, though not one of the most elabo-
rate, is one of the longest and most thoroughly developed in
all Bach's writings. It is constructed on two subjects, which,
together with subsidiary matter, are freely worked both
separate and in conjunction. The first is as follows :—

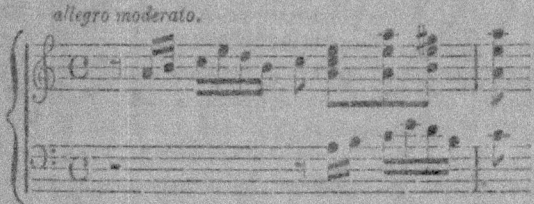

The second as below :—

* One of the three existing manuscript copies in the library
of Forkel bore that date, and thus fixed the extreme limit of the
time at which the composition could have been written—that is to
say, exactly a quarter of a century before Bach's death.

Some idea of the manner in which they are elaborated may be gathered from the subjoined :—

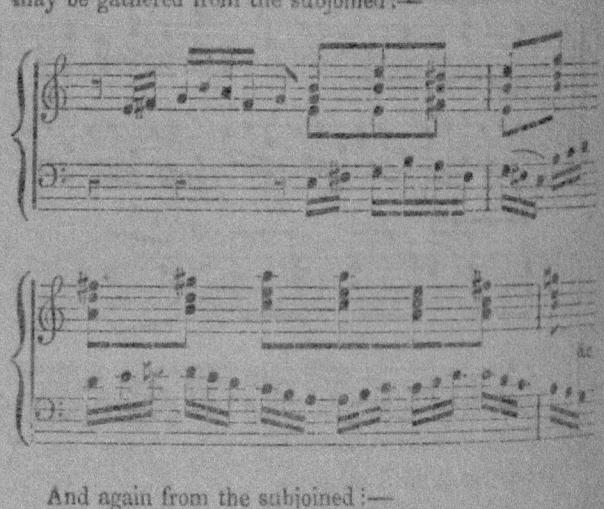

And again from the subjoined :—

An episode is worth noting, which at first appears in C, the relative major of the primary key :—

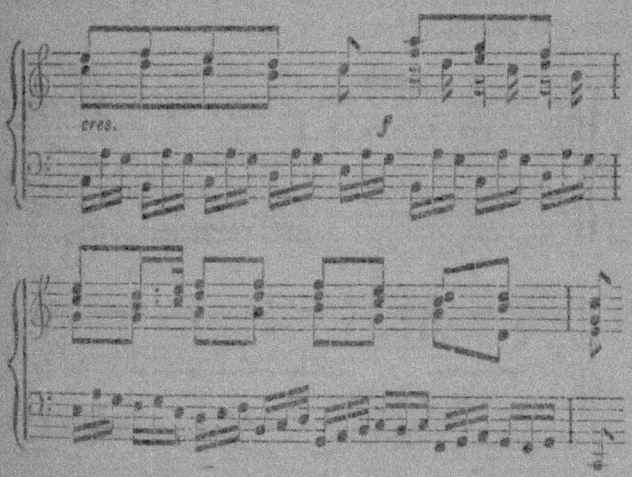

And further on in D minor :—

456

Then we have a sort of *bravura* passage, which suddenly interrupts the development of the theme, only to lead back to it :—

This re-occurs in another shape, and bringing back the theme in another key :—

The most striking and remarkable form this subsidiary *bravura* assumes, however, is when again interrupting the course of the regular development, it gives may to the final appearance of the leading theme: —

158

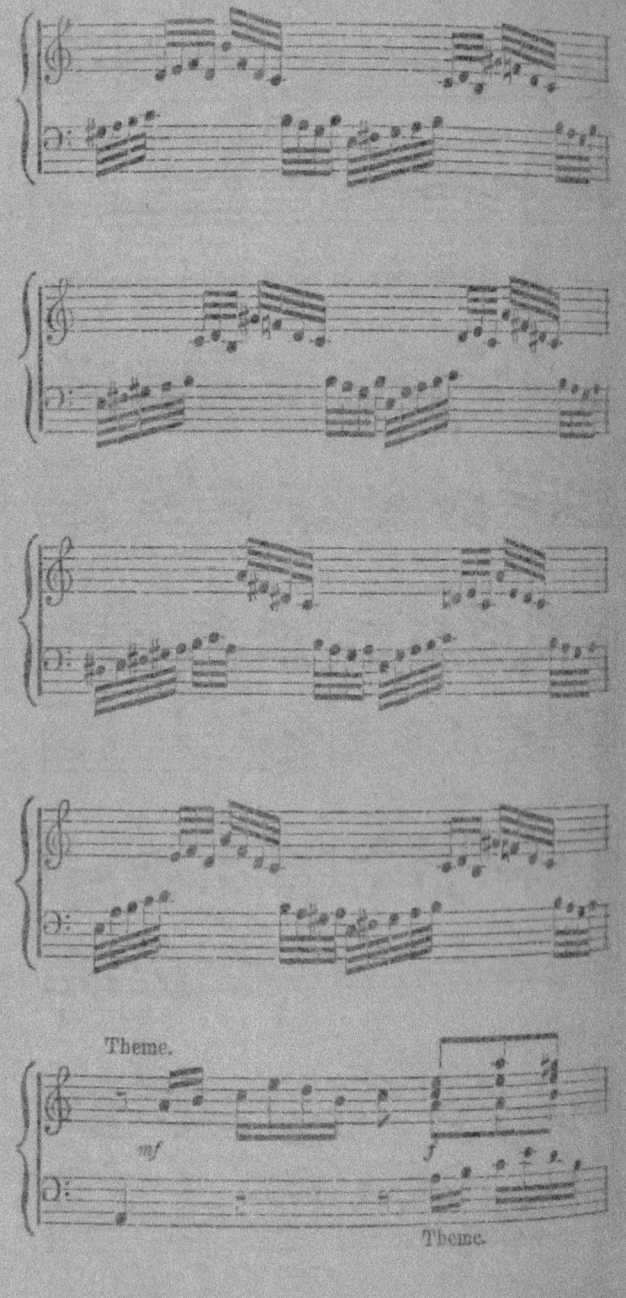

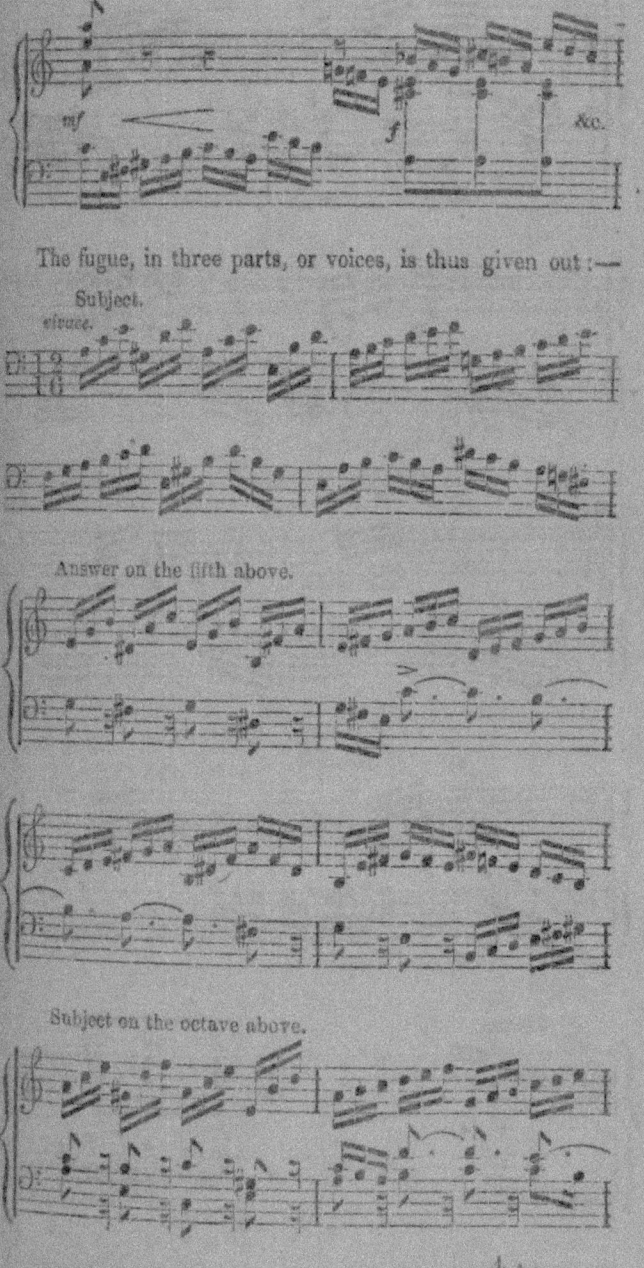

The fugue, in three parts, or voices, is thus given out:—

Subject.

Answer on the fifth above.

Subject on the octave above.

4 A

The leading subject never ceases to appear, in one form or another, from the beginning to the end of the fugue; so that further quotation would be superfluous. Except, perhaps, the fugue at the end of Beethoven's Grand Pianoforte Sonata in B flat, Op. 106, no similar composition for the pianoforte of equal brilliancy exists.

The Prelude and Fugue (alla Tarantella) in A minor, were first introduced by Madame Arabella Goddard, at the seventh concert of the third season—January 14, 1864.

END OF THE FIRST PART.

_{*} Madlle. MARIE KREBS will perform on one of Messrs. JOHN BROADWOOD and SONS' Concert Grand Pianofortes.

SATURDAY POPULAR CONCERTS, ST. JAMES'S HALL.— On Saturday afternoon, January 16, the Programme will include Mozart's Quintet in C minor, for Stringed Instruments; Beethoven's Pianoforte Trio in C minor; Largo and Allegro by Marcello, for Violoncello; and Beethoven's Sonata Appassionata, for Pianoforte alone. Executants, Mdlle. MARIE KREBS, MM. STRAUS, L. RIES, ZERBINI, BURNETT, and PIATTI. Vocalist, Miss ANNIE SINCLAIR. Conductor, Sir JULIUS BENEDICT. To commence at Three o'Clock.

Subscription Tickets, to the Sofa Stalls, for the 7 Morning Concerts, taking place on Saturdays, January 16, 23, 30, February 6, 13, 20, and 27, at £1 10s.

Sofa Stalls, 5s. Balcony, 3s. Admission, 1s. Tickets and Programmes at CHAPPELL & Co.'s, 50, New Bond Street.

Part II

GRAND TRIO, in B flat major, Op. 97, for Pianoforte,
Violin, and Violoncello.   *Beethoven.*

(Twentieth performance at the Popular Concerts.)

Allegro moderato—B flat major.
Scherzo, Allegretto—B flat major; with Trio—B flat minor.
Andante cantabile—D major.
Allegro moderato—B flat major; with Presto—D major and
B flat major.

Madlle. MARIE KREBS, Herr STRAUS, and Signor PIATTI.

This great work—the sixth and last of Beethoven's piano-
forte trios—was dedicated by the composer to the Archduke
Rodolphe, upon whom he conferred so many similar favours,
and among others the sonata in G, for pianoforte and violin,
Op. 96, the work which immediately preceded the Trio in
B flat (as the *Lieder Kreis*, Op. 98—dedicated to Prince
Lobkowitz, Duke of Raudnitz, to whom, so many years pre-
viously, the first six Quartets, Op. 18, had been inscribed—
immediately followed it) in the order of publication. The
Trio, produced shortly after the Pastoral Symphony, and
therefore coming before the last three symphonies, the later
sonatas, the Mass in D, and the last five quartets, is one of
the brightest and most splendid examples of Beethoven's so-
called "Second Period," at its zenith. The leading themes
of each movement are appended:—

Allegro moderato (first theme).

(Second theme.)

Scherzo.

(Tributary.)

Trio.

(Tributary.)

Andante cantabile.

This wonderfully rich movement is in the variation form, of which Beethoven has given more (and more magnificent) examples than any other composer—Bach and Mozart not excepted.

Allegro moderato (Finale).

4 B

468

(Second theme.)

On the title page of the original MS. (in possession of Herr Paul Mendelssohn, brother of the celebrated composer), is found, in Beethoven's handwriting, at the beginning—" Trio am 3ten März, 1811. Beethoven ;" and at the end—"il fine—geendigt am 26ten März, 1811."

The Trio, Op. 97, was first introduced by Herr Nicolas Rubinstein, M. Wieniawski, and Signor Piatti, at the twenty-first concert of the third season—June 10, 1861.

SONG, Miss EDITH WYNNE.

(*Faust.*)   *Gounod*

Versar nel mio cor il tuo duolo!
Puoi chè l'amor s'assopi,
La fiamma spari, resta solo,
L'affetto che nostr' al me uni.

Si spense d'amor la scintilla!
Duolo ho nel cor non amor,
V'accolsi il pianto, stilla a stilla,
Che il tuo cor frantò versa ognor.

This song was composed expressly for Madame Nantier Didiée, the representative of the character of Siebel, in the Italian version of *Faust* given at the Royal Italian Opera.

———

AN INTERVAL OF FIVE MINUTES.

———

FANTASIA, in C major, Op. 159, for Pianoforte and
Violin. *Schubert.*

(Fourth performance at the Popular Concerts.)

Andante molto—C major.
Allegretto—A minor; leading to
Andantino—A flat major.
Tempo primo; leading to
Allegro—C major.
Allegretto—A flat major; leading to
Presto—C major.

Madlle. MARIE KREBS and Herr STRAUS.

The only reference we find to this piece is in the catalogue
of Schubert's compositions at the end of the biography of Dr.
Heinrich Kreisle von Hellborn:—"*Sonate für Clavier und
Violine* (1817)—*Autograf bei Diabelli, Oper* 159, oder
162." Even the key of the work is not mentioned. Thus,
as Schubert was born (at Vienna) in January, 1797, he was
in his 21st year when he composed it. Why it should be
styled "Sonata" it is difficult to explain, seeing that it is a
"Fantasia" in the strictest sense of the word. A mere
indication of the leading themes will suffice :—

Andante molto.

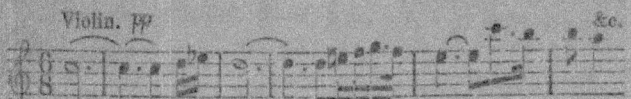

The above is ushered in by a few bars, "*Tremolando*,"
for the pianoforte, which accompanies the melody cited in the
same manner.

Allegretto (leading theme).

(Second theme—A major.)

Pianoforte.

Violin.

Andantino.

The above theme, though transposed a note lower, is identical with that of the familiar and beautiful *Lied*, set to Rückert's stanzas, "Sei mir gegrüsst"—published by Schubert four years later. The variations on this melody will speak for themselves.

We have now a reference to the introduction, already quoted; which leads directly to the *finale*.

Allegro (Finale).

When this is fully developed, the theme of Rückert's *Lied* appears again, in a newly varied form :—

allegretto.

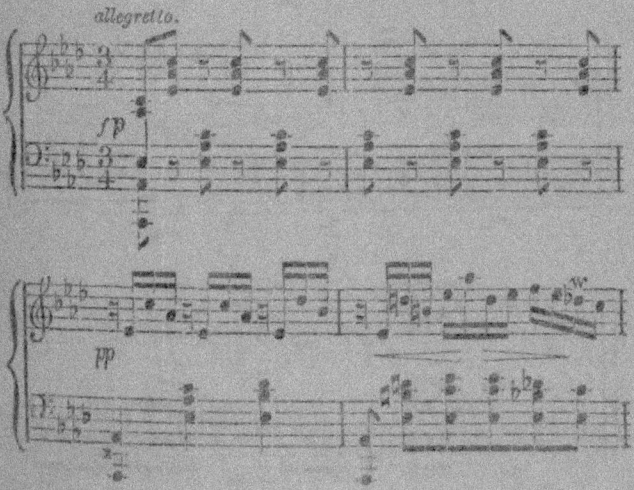

(Coda.)

The Fantasia in C major was first introduced by Mr. Charles Hallé and Herr Joachim, at the twenty-seventh concert of the tenth season—March 28, 1868.

———

END OF THE FOUR HUNDRED AND NINTY-EIGHTH

CONCERT.

———

J. MALLETT, PRINTER, 59, WARDOUR STREET, SOHO, LONDON, W.

SATURDAY POPULAR CONCERTS.

SATURDAY AFTERNOON, JAN. 16th, 1875.

PROGRAMME.

QUINTET, in C minor, for two Violins, two Violas, and
Violoncello ....Mozart.

MM. STRAUS, L. RIES, ZERBINI, BURNETT, and PIATTI.

SONG, "Let me wander not unseen." ....Handel.

Miss ANNIE SINCLAIR.

SONATA APPASSIONATA, Op. 57, for Pianoforte alone ... Beethoven.

Madlle. MARIE KREBS.

LARGO and ALLEGRO, for Violoncello, with Pianoforte
Accompaniment .... Marcello.

Signor PIATTI.

SONG, "Orpheus with his lute," .... Sullivan.

Miss ANNIE SINCLAIR.

TRIO, in C minor, Op. 1, No. 3, for Pianoforte, Violin, and
Violoncello ....Beethoven.

Madlle. MARIE KREBS, MM. STRAUS and PIATTI.

Conductor   -   -   Sir JULIUS BENEDICT.

4 D

www.ingramcontent.com/pod-product-compliance
Lightning Source LLC
Chambersburg PA
CBHW082052220626
47052CB00006B/1216